OLIVIA

I Can Do Anything!

by Natalie Shaw

Simon Spotlight
New York   London   Toronto   Sydney   New Delhi

Based on the TV series OLIVIA™ as seen on Nickelodeon™

SIMON SPOTLIGHT
An imprint of Simon & Schuster Children's Publishing Division
1230 Avenue of the Americas, New York, New York 10020
First Simon Spotlight paperback edition April 2016
OLIVIA™ Ian Falconer Ink Unlimited, Inc. and © 2016 Ian Falconer and Classic Media, LLC
SIMON SPOTLIGHT and colophon are registered trademarks of Simon & Schuster, Inc.
For information about special discounts for bulk purchases, please contact
Simon & Schuster Special Sales at 1-866-506-1949 or business@simonandschuster.com.
Manufactured in the United States of America 0316 LAK
1 2 3 4 5 6 7 8 9 10
ISBN 978-1-4814-5218-2
ISBN 978-1-4814-5219-9 (eBook)

Today was an important day for Olivia. Her dog, Perry, was about to graduate from dog-training school! She helped him practice what he had learned.

"Fetch!" Olivia ordered, and Perry fetched a ball.

"Roll over!" Olivia said, and Perry rolled over. "Good dog, Perry!"

Then Olivia put Perry's leash on him, and he wagged his tail with excitement. "Perry, heel!" Olivia said as they started walking, and Perry walked calmly without pulling on the leash. "I think you're ready to graduate!" she said, giving him a treat.

At the graduation ceremony Perry got to wear a special cap.

He looked as proud as Olivia felt.

"You did it, Perry! You graduated!" Olivia patted him on the head.

"I wonder what you'll do next!"

Now that Perry was a graduate, Olivia imagined that he could become a veterinarian who traveled the world helping other animals.

"I can see it now . . . ," she thought. "Dr. Perry would be the best dog doctor in the whole universe!"

That got Olivia thinking. What would she do when she graduated from school? She had liked training Perry so maybe . . .

Olivia imagined she would be an excellent lion tamer! If she was a lion tamer and Perry was a veterinarian, they could work together in a traveling circus!
"Pleased to meet you!" Olivia would say, teaching lions to shake hands, sit, stay, fetch, and roll over. "Good lion!"

Olivia also liked cooking, so perhaps she would become a chef!

She imagined having her own restaurant, Chez Olivia, where the food would be served on red dishes and people would come from all over to try her famous Super Sparkly Spaghetti!

"Bon appétit!" Olivia imagined saying to her guests.

Then Olivia thought about her favorite hobbies. She loved drawing, painting, and doing anything creative!

Olivia imagined being an artist, creating marble sculptures and painting priceless masterpieces. Maybe one day her artwork would be displayed in a big museum.

Thinking of painting reminded Olivia of another favorite hobby of hers: dancing!

Olivia imagined being a professional ballerina, performing in front of cheering audiences, wearing beautiful costumes, and curtsying to standing ovations every night!

But that wasn't all Olivia wanted to do when she grew up. She liked building model houses with her dad, and she wanted to become an architect, just like him.

Olivia imagined she was a great architect, building houses and skyscrapers and everything in between. And even if blueprints were blue, Olivia would always wear a red hard hat!

Thinking of cities reminded Olivia of how much she liked to travel and see new places.

She imagined she might like being a pilot with her own red plane someday, as the captain of Olivia Airlines.
"Ready for takeoff!" she would announce to the passengers, then fly into the clouds and land in wonderful destinations all over the world.

But why stop there? Olivia wondered. Thinking about traveling the world made her want to travel to outer space.

"The view is amazing!" Olivia the astronaut would say to Mission Control.

Olivia wanted to be so many things . . . and she kept coming up with ideas, like a star baseball player, and a magician.

"How will I ever choose just one thing to be when I grow up?" Olivia asked Perry. "One is just not enough!"

Perry barked and licked her face.

"You're right, Perry. I can do many things!" Olivia decided. "I don't have to pick just one!"

Olivia decided she knew just what she wanted to be when she grew up: She'd be Olivia the pilot/architect/magician/baseball player/ballerina/chef/artist who tames lions in her spare time!

After all, Olivia knew that she could do anything if she believed in herself and worked hard in school. But first she'd have to graduate, just like Perry!

Olivia smiled. There were so many possibilities for her. But for now she was happy to have her imagination . . . and a dog like Perry, even if he misbehaved sometimes!